Contents

Beowulf the Brave

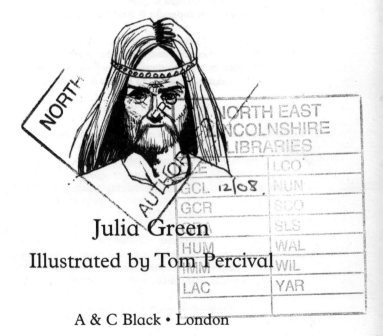

Julia Green

Illustrated by Tom Percival

A & C Black • London

White Wolves Series Consultant: Sue Ellis,
Centre for Literacy in Primary Education

This book can be used in the White Wolves Guided Reading programme
with more experienced readers at Year 3 level

First published 2008 by
A & C Black Publishers Ltd
38 Soho Square, London, W1D 3HB

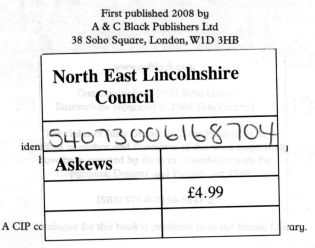

www.acblack.com

Text copyright © 2008 Julia Green
Illustrations copyright © 2008 Tom Percival

iden... ...ber and... ...work respecti...
...rted by the... in accordance with the
...pyright, Designs and Patent Act 1988.

ISBN 978-0-7136-8841-2

A CIP catalogue for this book is available from the British Library.

This book is produced using paper that is made from wood
grown in managed, sustainable forests. It is natural, renewable and
recyclable. The logging and manufacturing processes conform
to the environmental regulations of the country of origin.

Printed and bound in Great Britain
by CPI Cox & Wyman, Reading RG1 8EX.

Chapter One

"Listen well: this is a story of brave deeds and horrific monsters, a story told around the fire in the dancing shadows over hundreds of years."

My name is Beowulf, after the bee-hunting bear – because I am brave, like a bear, with wolf-grey eyes and fair hair. It's a good name for me: all my life I have needed to be brave.

My story starts with a journey from my country, Geatland, across the seas where the whales ride, where the swans sail, all the way to Denmark.

The king there was in trouble. His people lived in terror. A fearful monster – part sea-wolf, part man-wolf – stalked their land. Every night, it came up from its sea-lair, and stole across the marshes in the darkness, leaving a trail of blood and death. It killed many men. They called the monster Grendel.

Long ago, the king of Denmark had been a good friend to my

father. Now, it was my duty to help him.

Fourteen brave warriors crossed the sea with me to take up the challenge: to kill the monster. We loaded our boat with spears and shields. The sun glinted on the shiny metal.

Our dragon-headed boat
skimmed through the waves,
pulled by the dipping oars.
Above us, the striped, square
sail billowed in the breeze.

"Land ahead!" someone
shouted at last.

As we got closer to the shore,
the wind dropped and the sail
flapped. We rowed into a bay
and landed on the pebbly beach.

A man on a horse came
trotting down from the headland
to meet us.

"Stop there!" he called. "Who
are you? What do you want?"

"I am Beowulf, from the land of the Geats, across the sea. Your king Hrothgar once helped my father. Now we have come to help him in return."

The man nodded his head. "This is good news. We have waited a long time for brave warriors like you. Come, I will take you to the king."

We followed him on foot, up
a small track through rough grass,
and over the marshes and down
through a forest, until we came
to a paved road. At last we saw
buildings. There were small huts,
fields, an orchard. People stopped
their work to watch us pass. We
walked on.

Finally, we arrived at a huge,
high building. It was the Great
Hall of Heorot, decorated with
the gilded antlers of a stag.

We smelled roast meat. We
heard voices. We left our spears
and shields at the door, and

went inside. Fires blazed in three
hearths. Long, wooden tables were
covered with food. The walls were
brightly decorated with woven
hangings and spears, and tusks
of walrus and narwhal.

A hush fell over everyone as we walked through the hall, towards the top table, to the king. The guard explained who we were.

"Welcome, Beowulf," said King Hrothgar. "You are brave to make this journey, but think hard before you take up the challenge. Many have tried and failed to kill the monster. Many noble warriors have died. Grendel is stronger than any human. Ordinary swords seem powerless against him. You will need all your strength and all the courage in your heart to defeat the shadow-monster."

"I have already made up my mind," I said.

"In that case, I accept your help with thanks. Now, let us share a feast and tell stories until night falls."

As it began to get dark, a shadow seemed to descend over

the hall. This was the moment everyone dreaded. People started to leave, going back to the safety of their own homes. Soon, only my brave warriors and I were left in the Great Hall.

We bolted and barred the heavy, wooden door. The fire died down to a glow. Candles flickered and burned low. We lay down and tried to sleep. My heart beat fast. How many hours would it be before Grendel came?

Chapter Two

One by one, my warrior friends fell asleep. I alone lay listening out for the first faint footfall as the monster crawled out of his sea-cave, crossed the wet moorland, crept closer through the thick mist.

I heard him snuffling at the locked door. He scraped the wood with his huge talons. With a terrible shriek, Grendel burst the lock and the doors swung open.

His huge bulk filled the doorway,
a black, hulking shadow. Everyone
was awake now, hands clasping
our swords even though we had
been told that they were powerless
against the Evil One.

With one swift move, Grendel snatched up the nearest man from the bench and bit off his head.

Horrified, I grabbed the monster's forearm with both hands and gripped it so tightly he writhed in pain.

My anger made me strong. It was a fight for life, me against the monster. For hours we struggled, his might against mine. I held him tighter, dodging his claws and his terrible teeth.

We crashed into tables and benches; the Great Hall rang with the clatter of plates and goblets as they were sent flying. The air stank of freshly spilled blood and the foul breath of the monster.

Like a caged animal, Grendel struggled to be free. He shrieked with despair. In one last, desperate move, he heaved his shoulder and twisted off his arm completely, leaving it in my hand. Howling, he disappeared into the night.

I collapsed, exhausted. But I had achieved my goal. Not even Grendel could survive such a terrible wound. He would surely die on the way back to his sea-lair. My warrior friends hung the arm from a hook on the wall as a battle trophy. Together, we grieved for the man he had killed.

At dawn, light stole over the land, and the Danes came back to the Great Hall to find out what had happened.

"We will celebrate in style tonight," said Hrothgar. "You are a hero, Beowulf, brave as a bear. Thank you."

Women brought fresh rushes for the floor of the Great Hall. They hung clean banners on the walls, and carried in new benches and tables. Order was restored.

Some of the men followed the blood-trail left by the dying monster, over the hills and moors and out to the cliffs. They found the sea near the caves red with Grendel's blood.

That evening, we drank sweet honey-mead and ate tasty roast meats with delicious herb bread as we swapped stories round the fire. The Danes gave us each a decorated sword as a present. The queen brought me more special gifts: a jewelled collar and a chain-mail tunic as fine as silk.

That night, the Danes slept in their Great Hall again, and my men and I stayed at the guest house in the village. Little did we know what would happen while we were sleeping.

Chapter Three

I was woken the next morning
by shouting.

"Wake up!" a Danish warrior
yelled. "Come quickly!"

He explained to us how
Grendel's sea-wolf mother, mad
with grief, had followed the
blood-trail back to the Great Hall
of Heorot in the dead of night.
There, she had killed one of the
best Danish warriors and snatched

back Grendel's arm from where
it hung on the wall.

"Saddle the horses," I said.
"We must ride out to the sea-caves
and kill Grendel's mother. Until
then, no one will be safe."

We followed the sea-wolf's
tracks across the dark moorland,
up paths so narrow we had to ride
single-file, along the cliffs and,
finally, down into a steep gorge.
At last, we arrived at the water's
edge. Spray lashed the rocks.
The sea churned and boiled. A
thick mist surrounded us. The air
seemed full of shadows and ghosts.

My men fell silent. They knew
I had to do this alone.

They helped
me put on my fine,
chain-mail tunic and
glittering gold helmet.
I took the ancient sword

I call Hrunting in one hand. It has
a blade of iron, sharp and true.
Then I dived into the sea.

Down, down I plunged for
what seemed like hours. I fought
off fierce sea-creatures with tusks,
wrestled through weed, slithered
past silent shoals of silvery fish.
Finally, I reached the seabed
and the entrance to the
sea-wolf's cave. Heart
thumping, I crawled
through a tunnel of
rock and found
myself on a tiny
beach of silver sand.

Out from the shadow came
the angry sea-wolf. She sunk her
jaws into my shaking body, but
my tunic protected me from her
terrible teeth.

I tried to stab her with my trusty sword, but it was powerless against her. I had to fight her bare-handed, like I had done with Grendel. We struggled for hours. She was even stronger than her son.

A shaft of sunlight glinted on an ancient dagger hanging on the sea-cave wall. In a last, desperate effort, I grabbed it and brought it crashing down on the sea-wolf's head. As if by magic, the dagger pierced her leathery skin and sliced into her skull. Finally, Grendel's mother fell back, dead.

Wearily, I turned. In the thin beam of light, I saw the corpse of Grendel slumped in the corner of the cave.

I used the magic dagger one more time, to hack off Grendel's head. Blood gushed out and at once the dagger blade seemed to dissolve, like melting ice.

I crawled back through the tunnel and swam up to the surface, Grendel's head under one arm.

As I appeared, my men shouted with joy. "When we saw the blood, we thought you must be dead. We almost gave up hope!"

"But you still waited," I said. "You are brave, loyal friends."

We carried Grendel's head high on our spears, back to the Great Hall of Heorot.

And another night of feasting and celebration began, with food and wine, storytelling and songs.

Chapter Four

Our job was finished. The next
morning, we returned to the beach
where we had left our war-boat,
and loaded up all the gifts of
gold and fine weapons the Danes
had given us. At last, we set sail
for home.

For two days we travelled, our
striped sail billowing in the wind.
Like whales, we followed the sea-
roads until, finally, we glimpsed

land. High on the cliffs of our
country, the coastguard was
watching for our safe return. By
the time we ran the boat ashore,
crowds had gathered on the beach
to welcome us home.

That night, we told the story of the battles with the monster Grendel and his sea-wolf mother, and showed off our treasures. I took my place again as chief warrior.

Many years passed. Kings came and went. Hrothgar, king of the Danes, died and his son ruled instead. In Geatland, our king Hygelac was killed at war, and his son Headred ruled our land. When he died in battle, the kingship was offered to me, and I accepted.

I, King Beowulf now, ruled the Land of the Geats for fifty

summers, fifty winters. All was well. I grew old, my hair turned silver-grey, like wolf fur.

Then trouble came again.

A dragon started to prowl the land, burning crops and houses with its fiery breath.

For years, unknown to us, it had lived hidden deep in a cave in the hills, guarding a treasure hoard of gold and precious jewels that had been left there hundreds of years before.

One day, it seems, a man stumbled across the cave by chance, and found the dragon's treasure. While the fire-dragon was sleeping, the man stole one golden goblet.

As soon as the dragon woke up, it knew something was missing.

It smelled the man. It found his footprints.

It spread its wings to fly after him.

Now, night after night, the angry dragon came looking for its stolen treasure. It left a trail of burned fields and houses.

One night, our Great Hall was scorched and ruined. Everyone was terrified.

I knew I must act bravely one more time. I must save my people from this new evil. But I also knew I was older now, and had little to protect me from a dragon's fire.

I asked the blacksmith to make me a special shield of iron. I chose twelve warriors to help me. Then I forced the thief who had brought this misery on us all to show us the way to the fire-dragon's lair.

The journey took two days, over hills and through dense woodland, up over the scorched moorland, past the blackened stumps of burnt trees. Finally, we arrived at the desolate place.

"There, where smoke curls like mist. That is the dragon's den," the thief told us. "It is full of gold and treasure."

I stepped forward. "Even though I am old I must fight this battle alone, as your king."

"Please let me come with you," said one brave young warrior, called Wiglaf.

"No," I told him. "This is a fight for one man, just like my battle with Grendel. But stay here and watch out for me."

I took the heavy, iron shield in one hand and my sword in the other, and walked slowly down the hillside, into the shadows. My heart beat fast with fear.

Chapter Five

The cave was dark, the air full
of smoke. I choked in the bitter
fumes. A stream trickled out at
one side, its water bubbling and
steaming. I held the shield before
my face and ventured
in, calling out to
wake the dragon.
It uncoiled and
yawned, sending
fire shooting out.

When it saw me, the dragon
sprang forwards, wings
outstretched. Its scales of gold
and greeny-blue shimmered
and flashed in the light from
its flaming breath.

I lunged at it with my sword.
Again and again, I tried to pierce
the scaly skin. Each blow sent
me reeling back from the
terrible heat. My hair
and face were
scorched.

Wiglaf, the brave young warrior, watched me from the hill top. I heard him clattering down towards the cave.

"Beowulf, I cannot bear to stand and watch any more. I'm coming to help you!"

His voice made the dragon rage. It spat fire.

"Quick, shelter with me behind the iron shield," I called to Wiglaf.

His wooden shield was no protection from the dragon's fire.

I swung my sword and crashed it down on the dragon's head, but the weapon shattered into tiny pieces. The dragon sprang again, talons slashing. Pain shot through my body.

Wiglaf seized his dagger and stabbed the dragon's soft underbelly. The dragon stumbled, its fire began to fade. I tugged my own dagger from my belt, and with the last of my strength I hacked its body almost in two. I staggered towards the mouth of the cave, towards the light, but my eyes were dim. I fell.

Wiglaf carried me out of the
cave and laid me on the soft grass.
He bathed my face with cool
water. Blood spurted from my
wounds. Wiglaf wept over my
battered body.

I did my best to comfort him.
"I am an old man. I have lived
a good life. There is no need for
sorrow. The dragon is dead.

My people are safe again, and the cave is full of gold and precious treasure to help you all. For this, I am glad." I took one last gulp of air. "When I am gone, make a special burial place for me high on the cliffs, so that seafarers will see the stones and remember me."

"That was the end of the life of the warrior-king, Beowulf. After his death, Wiglaf and his friends made a huge funeral fire. They took ten days to build a special stone burial mound, high on the windswept cliffs where the sea-birds wheeled and swooped.

They sang his death song, and celebrated his great life. They said there had never been a king like him. His bravery would never be forgotten. His story would be celebrated for generations, passed down through the centuries."

About the Author

Julia lives with her family in Bath.
When she's not writing stories or
helping other people write stories,
she likes camping by the sea,
long walks along the cliff tops, or
lazing in the garden with coffee
and cake. She's not at all brave
like Beowulf!

Her stories for younger readers
include *Over the Edge*, *Taking Flight*
and *Sephy's Story*.
Find out more at her website:

www.julia-green.co.uk

Year 3

Stories with Familiar Settings

Detective Dan • Vivian French

Buffalo Bert • Michaela Morgan

Treasure at the Boot-fair • Chris Powling

Mystery and Adventure Stories

Scratch and Sniff • Margaret Ryan

The Thing in the Basement • Michaela Morgan

On the Ghost Trail • Chris Powling

Myths and Legends

Pandora's Box • Rose Impey

Sephy's Story • Julia Green

Wings of Icarus • Jenny Oldfield

Arthur's Sword • Sophie McKenzie

Hercules the Hero • Tony Bradman

Beowulf the Brave • Julia Green